Produced by Kroha Associates, Inc.
Middletown, Connecticut

Printed in the United States of America.

ISBN 1-56326-162-6

Scared Silly

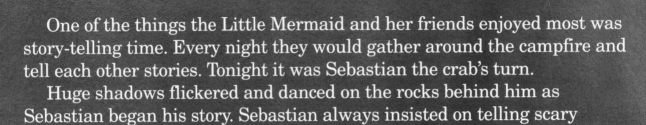

One of the things the Little Mermaid and her friends enjoyed most was story-telling time. Every night they would gather around the campfire and tell each other stories. Tonight it was Sebastian the crab's turn.

Huge shadows flickered and danced on the rocks behind him as Sebastian began his story. Sebastian always insisted on telling scary stories, and he said this was the scariest one of them all because it was true.

"Once when I was a little bitty crab," Sebastian began, "I was in the water right where Flounder and Sandy are now, when all of a sudden I felt something swim by my feet."

"The next thing I knew, this great big, hairy sea monster rose up out of the water and grabbed me!

"I fought with all my might to get free, but the monster was too strong. Finally, just as it was about to eat me, I pulled in my claws and slipped out of its grasp and swam away as fast as I could. I thought I had seen the last of that horrible monster, but — oh, no!"

"There it is now! Right behind you!" Sebastian shrieked.
Ariel gasped and whirled around to see what was there. Flounder and
Sandy both screamed.

"Hah, hah! I got you that time! You should have seen the looks on your faces!" the crab said, laughing so hard that his sides hurt.

"We weren't scared," Flounder said, trembling with fear.

"Oh, no?" Sebastian teased him. "You sure could have fooled me! You and Sandy jumped so high I thought for a minute you were a couple of flying fish! You were *all* scared!"

"And we're *all* leaving, too!" replied Scales the dragon.

"That's right," Ariel said. "How would you like it if we scared you — and then teased you about it?"

"Wait! It was only a story," Sebastian called out, but there was no one left to hear him.

"I wish Sebastian didn't always tell such scary stories," Scales said once he and Scuttle the seagull were safely back at Scales's cave.

"Me, too," said Scuttle, his voice still trembling. "I wasn't really scared, of course, but it isn't fair to the others. Somebody ought to teach that crab a lesson."

"Sebastian makes me so angry sometimes," Ariel said as she and Flounder and Sandy made their way home.

"Imagine," Flounder replied, trying to sound more brave than he felt, "thinking we were scared by a silly story."

Suddenly Sandy saw something up ahead. "Wha–what's that?" she asked. "Look out! It's the sea monster!" cried Ariel. But it wasn't really a sea monster, it was just an old bucket sitting in a clump of seaweed. "That gives me an idea," Flounder said.

The next day Flounder showed Ariel and Sandy how they could use the rusty old bucket and the seaweed to make a monster. Sandy stuck seashells on the sides as fish scales, and Ariel added two big sand dollars for eyes.

"Wow!" Sandy said when they were finished. "What a scary monster we made!"

"Now we can get even with Sebastian," said Flounder gleefully.

"Do you really think it will work?" Ariel asked.

"There's one way to find out," replied Sandy. "Here comes Sebastian now!"

Ariel and Flounder and Sandy quickly put on their monster costume. They were going to sneak up on Sebastian and tickle his feet. But by the time they were close enough to reach him, the crab had pulled himself up on a rock and was stretched out in the sun.

"What are we going to do now?" Sandy asked.

"Let's jump up out of the water and really give him a scare!" Ariel replied. "Ready? One...Two..."

"Three!" The friends jumped up into the air as high as they could. And got a terrifying surprise. There, towering above them was the biggest, meanest monster they'd ever seen!

It was as tall as a tree, and had a spiked tail that stretched out far across the sea. Right in the middle of its huge, ferocious-looking face were two eyes the size of coconuts, and a bright red mouth filled with sharp, pointy teeth.

"Aaaaggh!" roared the monster. Sebastian looked up at both monsters and was terrified.

Ariel and Flounder and Sandy were so frightened they threw off their costume and started to swim away as fast as they could.

But the big monster was just as afraid of Ariel and her friends. As *it* tried to get away, its spiked tail caught between the rocks and came loose — it wasn't a real monster after all! It was only Scales and Scuttle in a costume of their own!

"That sure was a scary costume you made!"
Ariel told Scuttle after everyone had
calmed down. "We thought you
were a *real* monster!"

"We were scared of you, too!"
said Scales.

"But we weren't trying to scare you," Flounder said. "We were only trying to scare Sebastian."

"So were we!" replied Scuttle. "We wanted to teach him a lesson."

"Hey, wait a minute," said Sandy. "Where *is* Sebastian?"

"H-h-h-here I am," the frightened crab replied in a tiny voice.

"I wish we hadn't tried to scare each other," Ariel said later. "Being frightened isn't funny."

"From now on, no more scary stories," replied Scuttle. "Right?"

"Right!" agreed Sebastian.

And so, that night, with the stars and the moon shining brightly, Ariel told them all a wonderful story about a princess and prince who fell in love and lived happily ever after. And best of all, no one got scared — not even once.